I'm Taller Than You!

First published in 2006 by
Franklin Watts
338 Euston Road
London
NW1 3BH

Franklin Watts Australia
Hachette Children's Books
Level 17/207 Kent Street
Sydney
NSW 2000

Text © A. H. Benjamin 2006
Illustration © O'Kif 2006

A CIP catalogue record for this book is available
from the British Library.

ISBN (10) 0 7496 6544 0 (hbk)
ISBN (13) 978-0-7496-6544-9 (hbk)
ISBN (10) 0 7496 6894 6 (pbk)
ISBN (13) 978-0-7496-6894-5 (pbk)

Series Editor: Jackie Hamley
Series Advisor: Dr Hilary Minns
Series Designer: Peter Scoulding

Printed in China

For Isabelle – A.H.B.

Franklin Watts is a division
of Hachette Children's Books.

I'm Taller Than You!

by A. H. Benjamin

Illustrated by O'Kif

W
FRANKLIN WATTS
LONDON • SYDNEY

A.H. Benjamin

"When I was young I was taller than all my friends. They used to call me Giraffe!"

O'Kif

"When I started drawing this book, I asked myself how things might look from above. I think they probably look very different!"

"I'm taller than you,"
Giraffe says to Tortoise.

"I'm taller than you,"
Giraffe says to Monkey.

7

"I'm taller than you,"
Giraffe says to Hyena.

"I'm taller than you,"
Giraffe says to Zebra.

11

"I'm taller than you,"
Giraffe says to Hippo.

"I'm taller than you,"
Giraffe says to Elephant.

"I'm taller than *all* of you!" Giraffe says to everyone.

"No you're not," they all reply.
"We are taller than you!"

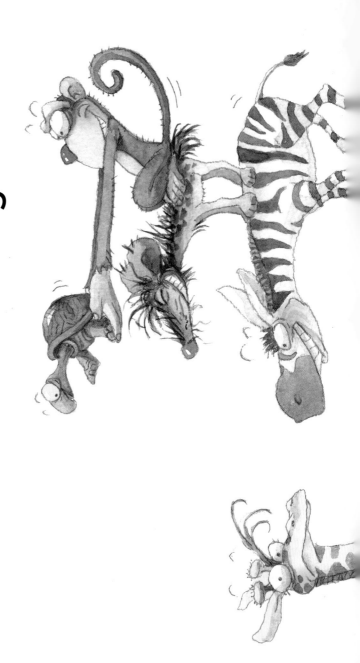

19

But they are not taller for long!

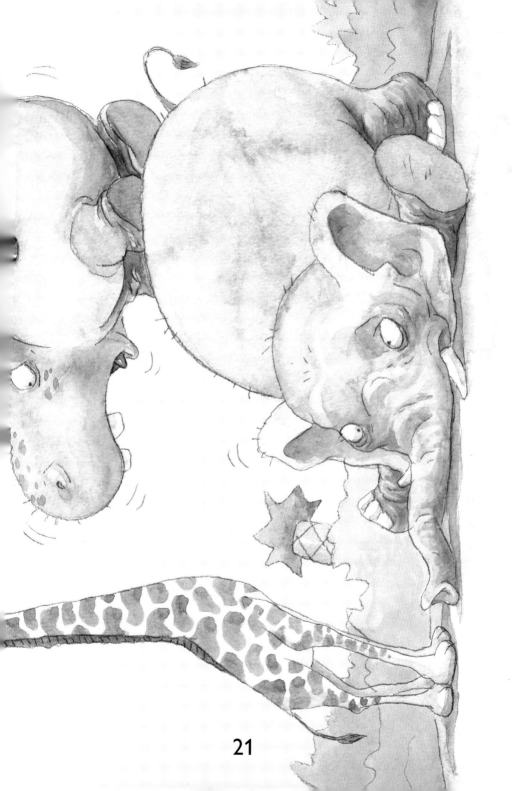

"I'm taller than you!" says Giraffe.

Notes for adults

TADPOLES is structured to provide support for newly independent readers. The stories may also be used by adults for sharing with young children.

Starting to read alone can be daunting. **TADPOLES** helps by providing visual support and repeating words and phrases. These books will both develop confidence and encourage reading and rereading for pleasure.

If you are reading this book with a child, here are a few suggestions:

1. Make reading fun! Choose a time to read when you and the child are relaxed and have time to share the story.

2. Talk about the story before you start reading. Look at the cover and the blurb. What might the story be about? Why might the child like it?

3. Encourage the child to reread the story, and to retell the story in their own words, using the illustrations to remind them what has happened.

4. Discuss the story and see if the child can relate it to their own experience, or perhaps compare it to another story they know.

5. Give praise! Remember that small mistakes need not always be corrected.

If you enjoyed this book, why not try another **TADPOLES** story?